EXTERIORS

ALSO BY ANNIE ERNAUX

EXTERIORS
ANNIE ERNAUX

Translated by
Alison L. Strayer

SEVEN STORIES PRESS
New York · Oakland

Seven Stories Press
140 Watts Street
New York, NY 10013
www.sevenstories.com

College professors and high school and middle school teachers may order free examination copies of Seven Stories Press titles. Visit www.sevenstories.com/pg/resources-academics or email academics@sevenstories.com

Library of Congress Cataloging-in-Publication Data is on file.

ISBN: 978-1-64421-097-0 (paperback)

Printed in the USA.

9 8 7 6 5 4 3 2

AUTHOR'S PREFACE

For the last twenty years I have lived in Cergy-Pontoise, a new town forty kilometres outside of Paris. Before that, I had always lived in the French provinces, in cities bearing the signs of history and the past. To find myself in a place suddenly sprung up from nowhere, a place bereft of memories, where the buildings are scattered over a huge area, a place with undefined boundaries, proved to be an overwhelming experience. I was seized with a feeling of strangeness, incapable of seeing anything else but the windswept esplanades, the concrete facades, pink or blue, and the empty residential avenues. I felt I was continually hovering in some no man's land halfway between the earth and the sky. My gaze resembled the glass surfaces of office towers, reflecting no one, just the high-rise buildings and the clouds.

I gradually emerged from this state of schizophrenia. I began to enjoy living there, in a cosmopolitan district, in the midst of lives started elsewhere—in Vietnam, in the West Indies, in the French provinces or, as was mine, in Normandy. I watched children playing at the foot of the tall buildings; I watched people strolling down the indoor galleries of the Trois-Fontaines shopping mall or waiting under bus shelters. I paid attention to the conversations exchanged in the RER. I felt the urge to transcribe the scenes, words and gestures of unknown people whom one meets once and whom one never sees again; graffiti hastily scribbled on walls and erased; sentences overheard on the radio and news items read in the papers. Anything that, in some way or another, moved me, upset me or angered me.

Looking back, I can now see a link between this enterprise and the Alzheimer's disease my mother was suffering from: her memory began to fail, she no longer recognized the people around her. This annihilation of her personality threw me into a state of utter confusion. I feel that writing about the outside world helped ease my grief and keep me in touch with the world that was gradually slipping away from my mother's own consciousness.

And so *Exteriors* was born—a diary which I kept up to 1992, and even up to the present day. It is neither reportage nor a study of urban sociology, but an attempt to convey the reality of an epoch—and in particular that acute yet indefinable feeling of modernity associated with a new town—through a series of snapshots reflecting the daily routine of a community. I believe that desire, frustration and social and cultural inequality are reflected in the way we examine the contents of our shopping cart or in the words we use to order a cut of beef or to pay tribute to a painting; that the violence and shame inherent in society can be found in the contempt a customer shows for a cashier or in the vagrant begging for money who is shunned by his peers—in anything that appears to be unimportant and meaningless simply because it is familiar or ordinary. Our experience of the world cannot be subject to classification. In other words, the feelings and thoughts inspired by places and objects have nothing to do with their cultural content; thus a hypermarket can provide just as much meaning and human truth as a concert hall.

I have done my best not to express or exploit the emotion that triggered each text. On the contrary, I have sought to describe reality as through the eyes of a photographer and to preserve the mystery and opacity of the lives I encountered. (Later on, in New York, when I came across Paul Strand's photographs of the inhabitants of the Italian village of Luzzano—powerful, almost painfully intense pictures; the stark characters are simply *there*—I believed this was the ideal vision of writing; inaccessible.)

In actual fact, I realize that I have put a lot of myself into these texts, far more than originally planned—memories and obsessions subconsciously dictating my choice of words and the scenes I wished to freeze. Moreover, I am sure that one can learn more about oneself by embracing the outside world than by taking refuge in the intimacy of a diary—a genre which appeared barely two hundred years ago and which may well disappear. It is other people—anonymous figures glimpsed in the subway or in waiting rooms—who revive our memory and reveal our true selves through the interest, the anger or the shame that they send *rippling* through us.

I love the soft burbling of streams and the cherry trees in blossom. But I agree with Plato when he makes Socrates say that he has nothing to learn from trees, only from men in the city.

A.E.
Cergy-Pontoise
May 1996

NOTRE *VRAI* MOI

N'EST—PAS

TOUT ENTIER

EN NOUS

JEAN-JACQUES ROUSSEAU

1985

On a wall in the covered parking lot at the RER station someone had written: INSANITY. Further along, on the same wall, I LOVE YOU ELSA and, in English, IF YOUR CHILDREN ARE HAPPY THEY ARE COMUNISTS.

Tonight, in the neighborhood known as Les Linandes, a woman went by on a stretcher held by two firemen. She was propped up, almost sitting—calm, with gray hair, aged between fifty and sixty. A blanket concealed her legs and half her body. A little girl said to another, "there was blood on her sheet." But there was no sheet over the woman. She crossed the marketplace of Les Linandes in this fashion, a queen among people rushing to shop at Franprix and children playing, until she reached the ambulance in the parking lot. It was half past five, the air was crisp and cold. From the top of a building that gives on to the square, a voice yelled: "Rachid! Rachid!" I put away the shopping in the trunk of my car. The man who collects the shopping carts was resting against the wall of the roofed-in passageway that connects the parking lot with the square. He was wearing a blue blazer and, as usual, gray trousers falling on to sturdy shoes. He has a striking expression. He came to retrieve my shopping cart when I had almost left the parking lot. To drive home, I took the road that runs along the gaping trench excavated to extend the RER. I felt I was riding toward the sun; it was setting beyond the criss-cross lines of pylons hurtling toward the center of the New Town.

In the train going to Saint-Lazare, an old woman settles in a seat near the aisle; she is talking to a young boy— possibly her grandson—who is still standing: "Why are you so restless? Whats wrong with where you live? A rolling stone gathers no moss." His hands are thrust deep into his pockets; he doesn't answer. After a moment, he says: "When you travel you meet people." The old woman laughs: "You'll see thin and fat ones anywhere!" Her face is beaming while she stares straight ahead, silent. The boy does not smile and examines his shoes, leaning against the wall of the car. Opposite them a handsome black woman is reading a Harlequin romance, *Love in Jeopardy.*

Super-M, in the Trois-Fontaines shopping mall, on a Saturday morning: a woman paces up and down the aisles of the "Household" section, clutching a broom in her hands. She is muttering to herself, looking distraught: "Where have they gotten to? It's not easy to get the shopping done when several people go together."

At the check-out area, there's a silent crowd. An Arab man keeps peering into his shopping cart, at the few articles lying at the bottom. Satisfied that the things he craved will soon be his, or afraid that he might have "overspent"; maybe both. A woman in a brown coat, in her fifties, flings her shopping on to the moving counter, grabs the articles after they have been rung up and tosses them back into the cart. She lets the cashier fill in her check and slowly signs it.

In the indoor galleries of the shopping mall, people circulate with difficulty. Without even looking at them, one manages to avoid the thronging bodies, barely centimeters apart. By unerring instinct or by habit. Only shopping carts and children bump into one's back or stomach. "Mind where you walk!" a mother cries out to her little boy. A few women in harmony with the lights and the mannequins displayed in shop windows—red lips, red boots, jeans hugging narrow hips, wild mane—stride by purposefully.

He got on at Acheres-Ville—twenty, maybe twenty-five years old. He settled across two seats, his legs stretched out, sideways. From his pocket he extracts a pair of nail clippers and uses them, contemplating the beauty obtained after treating each finger, extending his hand in front of him. The passengers around him pretend not to notice. Clearly, it's the first time he has owned a pair of nail clippers. Insolently happy. Nobody can mar his happiness—the happiness of a man with bad manners, or so the expressions of those around him would seem to suggest.

On the train, a little girl nags her mother to read a book in which each page begins with: "What time is it? It's time to . . ." (have lunch`, go to school, say goodnight, etc.). The mother reads through the book out loud. Then the little girl insists on reading it. But it's obvious she doesn't know how to; she has only learned by heart what her mother has read out to her (no doubt several times already) for she confuses the actions one is supposed to do at certain times. Her mother corrects her. The little girl repeats gleefully, louder and louder: "It's four o' clock, it's time to walk Baby; it's five o' clock, it's time to feed the cat," and so on. She gets more and more excited, and breathless, as she chants the relentless chorus of times and activities, imperatively linked. Now she's flustered, squirming in her seat, turning the pages of the book with something akin to fury, "what time is it it's time to." Normally, this frenzy of repetition, typical of children, is quick to climax, ending in shouts, tears and a slap on the face. In this case, the little girl hurls herself at her mother and says: "I want to bite you."

This Sunday morning, on the main square in Les Linandes, the greengrocer adjoining Franprix waters the lettuces in his stall with a small watering can. A sense of unease, as if he were peeing on them. He's a scrawny man in a blue coat, with a thin moustache. In the parking lot, the man who collects the shopping carts is standing against a wall. He must be in his late twenties. A guy walks up to him: "Want a smoke?" He moves away from the wall and takes the cigarette without removing his thick woolen gloves. He lights it with the other man's cigarette. It's a cold, raw day.

At the butcher's in the old village, at the foot of the New Town, customers are waiting to be served. When it was her turn, a woman said: "I'd like a steak for a man." Then the butcher asked: "Anything else?—No, that's all," she said, getting out her purse.

On the Mairie d'Issy subway line, a woman with a headscarf is scrutinizing the underground darkness through the window, as if she were traveling above ground, watching the fields and villages go by. Suddenly she addresses the woman sitting next to her: "Nothing but junkies, and they're mean too!" Her speech becomes indistinct. One can only catch, "you know, that Jewish minister who released everybody in prison."

For ages now, at La Samaritaine, in the Trois-Fontaines shopping mall, we have been hearing a man's voice urging us to buy up the whole store in various tones: quizzical, merry, threatening, playful: "It will soon be winter; you'll be needing thick, warm gloves and scarves. Come and see our new range of woolen accessories," or "Madame, has it ever occurred to you that the virtues of a perfect hostess are reflected in the choice of her tableware? In our china department . . ." A young, coaxing voice. Today the man belonging to that voice was surrounded by toys, a microphone in one hand. He's a red-head, half-bald, with huge, thick spectacles and small, greasy hands.

I bought a copy of *Marie-Claire* at the station in the New Town. This month's horoscope: "You will meet a wonderful man." Throughout that day I wondered if the man I was talking to was the one they meant.

(By choosing to write in the first person, I am laying myself open to criticism, which would not have been the case had I written "she wondered if the man she was talking to was the one they meant." The third person—he/she—is always some-body else, free to do whatever they choose. "I" refers to oneself, the reader, and it is inconceivable, or unthinkable, for me to read my own horoscope and behave like some mushy school-girl. "I" shames the reader.)

1986

The blind man at Saint-Lazare station was there. You start to hear him the moment you slip your ticket through the turnstile. A powerful voice, punctuated by wrong notes, on the verge of hoarseness. He always sings the same songs, the ones we learned at school or at summer camp, like *Là-Haut sur la Montague, l'Etait un Vieux Chalet* or *Je Ne Regrette Rien* by Edith Piaf. He holds himself perfectly straight, his head tilted back like all blind people, standing at the intersection of two corridors, just before the fork branching off to Porte de la Chapelle or Mairie d'Issy. In one hand, the white stick, in the other, a metal cup. A floppy dog lying at his feet. Quite often, among the people rushing by, someone, usually a woman, drops a coin into the cup, which clinks loudly. The blind man immediately stops singing and shouts

THANK YOU VERY MUCH HAVE A GOOD DAY, addressing no one in particular. All the passengers are aware that a good deed has been accomplished, a deed that will bring its author good luck. A perfect act of charity. A coin is given to a clean, dignified pauper—a tribute to yesterday's songs—in exchange for public recognition and the hope of being graced by fate throughout the day. Of all the poor men in the subway, he probably receives the most money. Today he was wearing a gray overcoat with herringbone motifs and a black scarf. I walked by at a respectable distance, like those who give him nothing.

The owner of an art gallery in the Rue Mazarine says to his visitor in a level voice, standing in front of a canvas: "Such a sensual painting." The woman heaves a deep sigh, as if overcome with despair by the statement, or incapable of bearing such a powerful emotion. Now they are conversing in low tones. The man, more distinctly: "See that red spot in the middle . . . quite extraordinary . . . who else would think of painting a red spot right in the middle . . ." The picture consists of a cracked-up ocher surface, possibly a representation of rocks in the sun. The title published in the catalog: "Ardèche, the red spot." I try to draw a parallel between my own conception of sensuality and what appears to be a barren landscape. But I do not possess the mental agility or sensitivity this requires. I realize that I have yet to be initiated into this area of knowledge. But then it is not a question of knowledge. After all, instead of saying "sensual," they might as well have used the word "refreshing" or "violent": the non-connection between the painting and its description would still be the same. It's all a matter of learning the right code. All the paintings in the gallery were priced between two and two and a half million old francs.

The lights and clammy atmosphere of the Charles-de-Gaulle-Étoile station. Women were buying jewelry at the foot of the twin escalators. In one corridor, on the ground, in an area marked out by chalk, someone had scribbled: "To buy food. I have no family." But the man or woman who had written that had gone, the chalk circle was empty. People tried to step around it.

Now there is a "Marcos Museum" in the Philippines (yesterday's edition of *Le Monde*). Visitors are shown round the palace that belonged to the former dictator and his wife. The official reason is to arouse indignation at such luxury and wealth but in actual fact satisfaction prevails: to feast one's eyes on the things one cannot afford and to be allowed to joke about them, to appropriate them both visually and verbally. The attention of the men and women who visit the "museum" focuses first, and almost exclusively, on the silk underwear of Imelda, the wife of President Marcos. The Revolution in this country ends there—in the sexual trappings of a woman, who moreover was hated. Five hundred brassieres, panties and suspender belts on show to be admired and touched; the women dream of wearing them, the men of jerking off inside them.

Super-M, on a Saturday. The cashier is old—older than the others, who are under twenty-five—and slow. The client—in her forties, thin-rimmed spectacles, an air of casual sophistication—asks for her receipt to be checked: it seems there's a mistake. It is necessary to call over a supervisor, the only person with the authority to record and then cancel the mistake using the cash register. The error is put right. The supervisor walks away. The cashier moves on to the next customer. The small lady with glasses, who is still there, busy checking her receipt, calls out to the cashier a second time: "There's still something wrong." The cashier leaves the customer she was dealing with. Further explanations are proffered by the little lady, who shows her receipt to the cashier. She takes it and stares at it blankly. She calls over the supervisor again. The little lady empties all her shopping out of the cart and the supervisor ticks off each item while the cashier returns to her client. When this operation is over, the supervisor turns to the cashier, shoving the ticket under her nose: "On the lady's receipt, there's 57F. None of the articles cost 57F. What's more, a pack of four radio batteries costing 17F isn't listed." The cashier says nothing. The supervisor insists: "Can't you see there's a mistake? Fifty francs." The cashier refuses to look at the supervisor. She is gray, tall and flat; her hands, which have left the cash register, hang limply on either side of her body. The supervisor repeats: "You must see there's a mistake!" All the clients waiting in line can hear her. Further along, the little lady awaits her due, expressionless under well-groomed hair. She stands as the proud, rightful consumer challenging the anonymous authority of Super-M. The old cashier, who has resumed her work in silence, is only a hand that is permitted no mistakes, be it in the interest of the store or the customer.

At the Academy of Music, housed in the arts center, a piano audition was under way. One after the other, the children climbed on to the stage, adjusted the stool, checked the position of their hands and launched into their piece. The parents, in tiered seats, were nervous and ill at ease. One little girl came to play in a long white dress with white shoes and a big bow in her hair. At the end of the audition, she gave a bouquet to the professor. It was like an old-fashioned dream come true in the heart of the New Town, with the rituals and pomp of yesteryear's salons. But the parents were not speaking to one another; each family wanted their own child to be the best, to fulfill the hope that one day he or she would belong to the elite, of which tonight they had witnessed only the theatricality.

        Opposite the rows of neat, tidy suburban houses, pink, cream-coloured, with green shutters (a little girl was opening a pair on the first floor and I could see plants and cane chairs through the bay window), separated from the urbanized area by a street bordered with lawns, starts an area of wasteland, with copses, a few derelict houses and a footpath with potholes filled with water. There are discarded objects everywhere, in the brambles and along the edges of the path. A paper wrapping for the Dutch cookies Spirits, a broken Coca-Cola bottle, cardboard packaging for a six-pack, a copy of the local gazette, a length of iron piping, flattened plastic bottles and a white substance with blisters—maybe sodden cardboard—suggesting a cluster of Sahara roses. Evidently, this desolate place is constantly frequented, but at obscure times, more likely at night.

Accumulated evidence of human company, of repeated loneliness. Traces of food, chiefly, although people tend to go there not to eat but to be alone, in groups of two or more. It's only natural to throw away paper wrappings and cans in this wild setting; to reclaim one's traces is the sign of a civilized superego.

Metamorphosis of all these objects, twice broken, rumpled and flattened—first by those who leave them behind, then by the bad weather. Combining two forms of wear and tear.

We are standing in front of the automatic teller in the shopping mall, forming a long line. A confessional without curtains. A panel slides open, we all repeat the same motions: wait, our head tilted to one side, press keys, wait, take our money, put it away and leave, avoiding other people's eyes.

The words "Your card is damaged" light up on the screen. I am stunned, at a loss to understand, as if I have been accused of some wrongful act unknown to me. I do not see why my credit card in particular should be damaged. Once again I perform the operations dictated by the computer. Once again: "Your card is damaged." The word "damaged" fills me with horror. I am the one who is damaged, the one to blame. I retrieve my card and leave without any money. I can understand people who vandalize cash machines, showering them with abuse.

On the freeway, level with the Marcouville high-rise apartments—a squashed cat, engraved into the asphalt.

As I leave the elevator in the underground garage, third level down, I am greeted by the rumble of air extractors. Nobody would hear a woman scream if she was being raped.

Memories as I am driving past the black 3M Minnesota office building with all its glass windows lit: when I first moved to the New Town, I would invariably lose my way but would go on driving, too panicked to stop. In the shopping mall, I would make sure I knew exactly through which door I had entered—A, B, C or D—so that I could locate the same exit later on. I would also try not to forget in which row of the parking lot I had left my car. I was afraid of having to wander under the concrete slab until nightfall without ever finding it. So many children got lost in the supermarket.

Only fucking matters, and, on a darker part of the wall, in red, *there are no inferior men.*

A free sheet with classifieds is slipped into my mailbox every week. "PROFESSOR SOLO-DRAMA. THE GREAT MARABOUT is among us at last. He offers to solve all our problems: unhappy love life, loss of affection, adultery, spells, poor academic results, bad sporting performances, departure of the loved one. If you want to be happy, don't waste any time: come and see me. Quick, professional service. Results guaranteed. 131B, Avenue de Clichy. 3rd floor. Right-hand door." (The photograph in the box shows a good-looking African.) In a few lines, a panorama of man's desires, a narrative written in the third person, then in the first. A character with a mysterious identity—a sage, maybe a magician—whose name conjures up poetry and drama. Two modes of writing, relying on psychology and marketing, respectively. A sample of fiction.

From an essay a student was reading on the RER, between Châtelet-les-Halles and Luxembourg, one sentence stood out: "Truth is related to reality."

Families and groups of youngsters were strolling down the galleries of the mall, slowly, in tightly-packed columns, amid the warmth and the lights. Very few people work between Christmas and New Year's Day so they come here in the afternoon. The winter sales have already begun. Although I only came here to buy coffee, after a few minutes, I find myself longing for coats, blouses, handbags; in other words, I see myself dressed in a twirling succession of coats and blouses. Black coats, for instance, despite the fact that I already have a black car coat. (But it's not the same, it's never the same; tiny differences between the models we crave and the ones we own: the collar, the length, the material, etc.) I succumb to a strange condition in which I want all sorts of clothes for myself, regardless of shape or color, in which I am seized with an overriding compulsion to buy a coat or a handbag. Once I am outside, this longing subsides.

In the luxury food store Hédiard, the salesgirl, a temp hired for the Christmas vacation, undid the gift-wrapping she had just finished. She wasn't sure she had put in the eight little pots of honey and jam. She wraps them up again, pinning down the package with one hand, while the other grabs a roll of adhesive Hédiard labels; she peels off one of these with her teeth. A woman entered the store, looking haughty. She pointed to the different types of ice cream she wanted for New Year's Eve, displayed in a refrigerated vitrine, "that one," "that one," then glanced around at the other customers, lightly, as if she could see through them. She ordered *foie gras* and said that today she needed a Poilâne loaf.

The Gérard Saint-Karl hairdresser's salon. For a long time I tried to figure out which of the men working here was Gérard Saint-Karl. I imagined he was probably the more mature, Apache-type man, still quite attractive. Later on, I noticed the photographs of men on the walls, and I believed I could detect a likeness between these men and the ones working in the salon, with their crew cut and their baggy pants. Recently, I realized that Gérard Saint-Karl was the name of a chain of hairdressers for men and women and that there was probably nobody called that at all. I felt I had been deceived.

All the girls in the salon have gotten on their party faces: bright make-up, heavy, sparkling earrings, red hair, blue streaks. They are the illustration of their own function and ambition: to turn each head into a nest of curls, scrolls, chips of jet and sunlight, the dazzling revelation of one day (by tomorrow the glamor will have worn off). Hairdressers of both sexes belong to a colorful, theatrical world; clad in the latest fashion, they also dress extravagantly outside of the salon. Six months ago the owner—the fake, still glamorous, Gérard Saint-Karl—had come to work as a cowboy, in a leather ensemble which revealed a band of bare midriff, suntanned, horizontal. Lately he came as a dancer, all in white, a vertical strip of flesh peeping through his shirt, open down to the waist. Today he has opted for Lawrence of Arabia, with a pair of black, loose-fitting pants, gathered in at the ankles, a white shirt, a scarf wound around his neck, a beard and long hair. A woman of about the same age, probably his wife, undergoes a parallel metamorphosis—tighter and tighter pants, larger and larger hoop earrings, false eyelashes—but a more predictable one, tending toward greater sophistication. He, in his Turkish pants, is well ahead of her.

The beautician hired before Christmas for make-up and waxing—a snappy dresser, going from one client to the next, offering her services and rates—was handing out plastic cups of coffee to the women waiting for their color to set. Later on, she swept away the locks of hair and took the clients' money. Nobody needed a facial.

"Do you think we got time to go to . . . (muffled)?
—What?

—You're going deaf!

—No, I'm not."

A strapping fellow of around eighteen is sitting opposite a woman, no doubt his mother, in the train going to Paris. Fleshy lips, small currant eyes.

"..........

—Eh?

—You see, you really are going deaf!"

She leans forward to grasp what he says. He is jubilant: "You're going deaf!" He has heavy thighs, spread wide apart under his raincoat, and is grinning triumphantly.

In a subway corridor, deserted in the middle of the afternoon, a man was leaning against the wall, his head bent forward. He was not asking for money. Drawing level with him, one noticed that his fly was open, revealing his balls. An unbearable sight—a shattering form of dignity: exposing one's masculinity. The women walking by avert their eyes. One cant possibly give him money, just pretend not to have seen him and harbor this vision until the train draws in. This sight stamps out everything else—the vanity of women in fur coats, the determined stride of market conquerors, the subservience of musicians and beggars to whom one gives the odd coin.

Why do I describe and detail this particular scene, like many others in the book? What is it I am desperately seeking in reality? Is it meaning? This may sometimes, though not always, be true since I have acquired the mental habit not only of experiencing emotions but of "getting them into perspective." Also, committing to paper the movements, postures and words of the people I meet gives me the illusion that I am close to them. I don't speak to them, I only watch them and listen to them. Yet the emotions they arouse in me are real. I may also be trying to discover something about myself through them, their attitudes or their conversations. (Sitting opposite someone in a subway car, I often ask myself, "why am I not that woman?")

The station at Port-Royal is undergoing restoration. The glass roof is encircled by boarding. From the platform you can still see the imposing, bourgeois façade of the Beauvoir Hôtel basking in the sun.

In the out-patient orthopaedics ward of the Hôpital Cochin, you must enter a cubicle one meter by one meter fifty, with a narrow bench and a peg for hanging clothes. On the far door, the one leading straight into the surgeon's consultation room, lies a sheet of paper with instructions. It explains how one should undress depending on which part of the body is going to be examined: upper garments for the shoulder, lower garments for the thigh. It's not clear whether visitors can keep on their shoes and panties, or whether they should remove all their clothes. There are three cubicles—A, B and C—each acting as a no man's land between the waiting room and the doctor's office. In one of these, a couple is whispering loudly. In a nagging voice, the man wonders what he should take off; the woman gives her opinion. You can also hear quite clearly the surgeon addressing the patient who has just been extracted from the cubicle (someone else has immediately taken her place). "How much do you weigh?—86 kilos." A pause. The surgeon is either thinking or manipulating the patient's limbs. Then he comments on the condition using medical terms, no doubt for the benefit of the interns and a secretary, whose typewriter can be heard. When the visit draws to an end, I begin to feel nervous. The cubicle door will open and I shall be exposed in my panties in front of four or five people. I freeze before daring to emerge and step forward into the brightly-lit room, like hens who remain huddled together at the back of their coop when the door is flung open.

At night, from the station platform at Saint-Lazare, you can see the lit-up windows of departing trains recede into the distance, then the red dots on the rear of the last car. Other trains emerge from the depths; you wonder which platform they are heading for, whether it will be the one where you are waiting, motionless, hemmed in by the crowd. Birds soar toward the crown of the glass cupola.

The man who collects the shopping carts for Franprix has gone. Now there are pay carts with a slot for coins.

At two adjoining check-out counters in the supermarket, two girls are chatting and laughing as they ring up the items, ignoring customers. It seems they're discussing a colleague who, in their opinion, mixes with dubious company: "Imagine my father's face if I brought home one like him!" The other one adds: "The worst thing is that she's not even ashamed!"

The President of the Republic spoke on television last Sunday. On several occasions he used the expression "little people" (believe this, suffer from that, and so on), as if the people he was referring to could neither see him nor hear him. I find it quite extraordinary for anyone to address a class of citizens on the assumption that they are inferior; even more extraordinary is the fact that they agree to be treated this way. The president's speech also implied that he himself was to be bracketed with "great people."

Ania Francos has cancer. She published "Chronicle of a Death Foretold" in *L'Autre Journal.* At the moment she is staying at a cancer hospital where she recently arrived to have a brain metastasis removed. She tells her story. She speaks about her little boy, who asked her, "will you live to see me grow up." It is impossible to *read* that. Normally, we see everything in relation to life. For Ania Francos, everything is seen in relation to death. Traveling on the RER, I read her words and her suffering: she is alive. In a few months, a few years, she will be dead. One can only read with that thought in mind. Ania Francos renders the other texts in *L'Autre Journal* meaningless.

Saturday, at the butcher's in the old village, at the foot of the New Town, near the Oise river. The butcher and his wife, along with their two assistants, a man in his fifties and a young lad, serve the many customers streaming into the store (people are jostling to get in). Mostly women, maybe a few couples with shopping baskets. More often than not, the butcher knows them by name; in fact, he and his wife say "Good Morning, Madame X" as soon as they catch sight of a familiar face, while continuing to serve another person. If they are dealing with occasional clients, or those who are not yet "regulars"—how long does it take to be accepted?—they remain distant and aloof, confining their conversation to the type and quantity of meat desired. The process is different with the established clientele. Time is taken over the choice, the customer runs her eye over the different cuts of meat displayed on the refrigerated shelf, "I'd like a fine sirloin steak," seeks advice, "is that enough for two?" The women take on drawling, almost dreamy tones to say "I'll have two veal escalopes"— an ode to domestic life, recited with satisfaction, peppered with graphic descriptions, "a piece of pork, to make a pot roast." It's a fair exchange: the butcher piling up the parcels of meat wrapped in waxed paper with his name on it is pleased to see the quality of his produce publicly acknowledged, as well as the money rolling in; the customer, for her part, is proud to show off her social status by naming and exhibiting the goods she consumes, and by demonstrating her ability to feed her family properly. When it's a couple, usually middle-aged, buying meat for the whole week, there's the satisfaction of showing that they are "well-off" or that they know how to entertain. Mutual recognition between the butcher and his client is conveyed by their hearty conversation and their joking. A subconscious ritual is being played out here, celebrating the convivial symbolism of meat, gorged with blood, the family and the recurring bliss of Sunday lunches. In a place like this, the young and the lonely, who ask for two slices of ham or some hamburger meat, and who have neither the time, the inclination nor the skill to prepare a stew, feel ill at ease. Painfully aware that they are both socially and economically inadequate when the butcher's question "Anything else?" is met by "No, that's all"; they prefer to shop in the supermarket.

A young girl, standing sideways, one hand clutching the grip of a seat, in a subway car running between Porte d'Orléans and Porte de Clignancourt. She is chewing gum vertically with fierce intensity, without pausing. A man watching her could only imagine her scissoring his penis and his balls.

On the Paris-Cergy train, at Nanterre station, a tall man sits down and joins his hands together on his knees. Then his hands start to shudder convulsively to rub against each other. The forefinger springs up, twitches in the air and returns to the other fingers. These hands show a white, even discoloration, such as that produced by certain acids. The man, an African, is completely still; only his hands move, incessantly, like squids. That too is the sign of an intellectual: never to feel the need to disassociate oneself from one's quivering hands, that have been damaged by work.

Le Monde, 7th March. The little girl is seated on a chair. She is held down by women: one locks an arm round her chest, another twists her arms from behind, a third women pries her legs apart. The matriarch in charge of excision slices off the clitoris with a knife or a shard of glass. She also cuts away the labia minora. The little girl screams, the women stop her from running away. There is blood everywhere. Women castrators, happy to perpetuate their condition of excised women. Devoted fairies gathered around the open belly, prematurely tearing out the moans of pleasure in an initial scream of pain.

The newspaper mentions that the practice of excision is dying out: now they only simulate the ceremony. The transition from reality to symbol is a form of release.

On the Cergy-Paris commuter line, two women seated opposite one another leaf through mail-order catalogs. The younger one ventures solemnly: "My mother never got over an incident that occurred in her building." Her companion looks up questioningly. The narrator therefore continues. She assembles the story in front of us (there are many passengers standing; several begin to listen), introducing a main character—an old lady with ulcerated legs—a place—the building where the narrator's mother lives—and a series of events: the old lady disappears, no sound is heard coming from her flat, then there is moaning, the mother tries to get the janitor to open the door, he refuses point-blank, so finally they call the police. The characters in the story are divided into "good" (the mother) and "bad" (the janitor). The tragic denouement can be inferred by the tone and the structure of the story; the young girl accumulates ominous details—"they couldn't break down the heavy door, it's an old building"—references to time—"the day before yesterday," "yesterday"—leading up to the horror of the present. She pauses, "so," then resumes the story, feigning surprise, "and suddenly," her tongue darting, her hand fluttering. Her pleasure at relating the incident is reflected in her face—eyes cast down, occasionally glancing at the very first recipient of the story, the young girl sitting opposite her (who has now become a fictitious figure, the real audience being the crowds of passengers crammed into the aisle of the subway car). The indecency of the description, the spectacle of the narrator's enjoyment, postponing the final twist, heightening the desire of the audience: all storytelling operates along the same lines as eroticism. They eventually discover the corpse of the old woman; she had been dead for a week.

(I realize that I am forever combing reality for signs of literature.)

The March sun beating down on the New Town. No density, just shadows and light—the parking lots blacker than ever, the dazzling concrete. A one-dimensional place. My heads hurts. I feel this condition allows me to penetrate the essence of the city—the white and remote dream of a schizophrenic.

Driving past the Pleyel high rise, near Saint-Denis. Impossible to say whether people live there or whether it is made up of offices. From a distance, it looks empty, black, malevolent.

In the newspaper *Libération,* the historian Jacques Le Goff remarked: "The subway is quite a curiosity." Would the people who commute every day feel the same way about the Collège de France? There is no way of knowing.

A television feature about the Maison de Nanterre. Elderly people, young girls and couples with children live here. They share an incapacity to fend for themselves, to work, to find accommodation, to plan the next day, the continuation of their life. They belong nowhere in the world except here. Refectories with tables for six, neat little bedrooms with flowered bedspreads. The generations merge: a twenty-year-old girl has come to join her mother, a fat blind woman. All experience a feeling of numb resignation. In the courtyard, a man collects all the stones he can find and arranges them to form rosettes around the trees. He says it's bad to leave the stones lying around. It's the last image of the film, accompanied by a voice-over: "This may be seen as a metaphor for the Maison de Nanterre—an establishment where order reigns supreme, where order is preserved." So, to find a fitting conclusion, they single out the gestures of one man—a chunk of his existence—and turn these into a symbol, a stylistic device. It stops you wondering why that man is there and why, despite the horror felt by both journalist and viewers at the prospect of living in such a place, other human beings are happy to be there, tucked away from the world.

At Saint-Lazare, a mother and her daughter settle opposite one another on the train to Cergy, talking in loud voices. The girl is reading and commenting on *Télérama*, "Gee! They're showing *The Cow and I*, with Fernandel!" and so on. The mother gets out some potato chips, "they're onion-flavored!" They both dip into the packet and finish them up. The mother: "When we get home, we're going to the supermarket.—No, I'm watching television.—Okay, do whatever you like." Clearly impressed by their own social status, they feel they have the right to share everything they do and say with the other passengers, knowing full well that they are the center of attention. They wish to act out the intimacy of a mother-to-daughter relationship which they see as enviable. They are both wearing sweat suits, white ankle socks and espadrilles, and are returning from the coast of Brittany.

From outside, the Leclerc hypermarket resembles a glass cathedral. Inside, you walk between huge shelves, separated by aisles, when suddenly, at the back of the store, behind a glass partition, you glimpse men and women dressed in white—coats, caps, plastic gloves—cutting up meat. Bloody carcasses hang from hooks. You feel that, after cramming your shopping cart with food, you have ended up at a hospital or a morgue.

An invalid was sitting in his wheelchair near the exit, laughing with the cashiers, who were ordering him to go and check the price of the articles with no bar code. He rests the packet against his stomach and propels himself toward the right shelves, then returns. The girls are amused by his performance, his eagerness to obey their orders. He is glad to be the center of interest of these pretty, teasing girls, delighted to have at their service a man whom they need never fear, whom they send whizzing back and forth on his wheels like a young puppy.

We were waiting at the dentist's, reading magazines laid out on a coffee table. Three patients who had never met. The sound of a motorbike close by reached us through the window of the waiting room (situated on the first floor). A young, male voice rang out, addressing someone from a distance: "So see you on Sunday, okay?" The reply, coming from a boy or a girl, was impossible to catch. "Don't be late, eh?" the voice continued. Then, much louder: "And good fuck with the principal!" No doubt said in jest, in lieu of "good luck." An embarrassed silence descended upon the waiting room, because of these words and the situation we were in—complete strangers unwittingly caught in the act of eavesdropping. Had we been alone, the incident might have amused or intrigued us. In the company of others, it became obscene.

The SNCF strikers on the television screen. During the demonstrations, they appropriate the songs and slogans from the students' strike a fortnight ago. They try to imitate them, as well as their language, "Take your pay plan and shove it!" When they are interviewed, they falter or use clichés coined by labor unions. In a subtle way, the media and the government treat them as inferior beings; the director of the SNCF affirms that "the first thing is to get the trains running; negotiations will come later," as if the workmen were dumb. The students' strike—"fun," imaginative people claiming free access to higher education—was staged by the rulers of tomorrow. The railroad workers' strike—"graceless" people clumsily demanding a little more money to live on—was staged by the ruled of today.

Over the phone, M—a redhead with spectacles, a fur coat in winter—in intellectual and peremptory tones: "We must get you a cat. All writers have cats.

Last week, J-C L, a literary critic, wrote: "The notebooks reveal the true writer." So writing is not enough; there need to be external signs, material evidence to define what a "real" writer is. Yet these signs are available to all of us.

1987

At Nanterre University, Madame A begins her lecture on the myth of Don Juan. "Today I shall talk about the ethics of the myth. What is the connection between myth and morality?" The students remain silent. "How would you define the ethics of the myth?" Still no answer. She insists: "Don't you have any idea?" She is wearing a raw silk blouse over pants—an elegant woman, on the slim side. Finally, she gives the right answer, in other words, the last link in a chain of arguments known only to her. "Morality is to go on existing." There is dismay among the students. They had hoped to be relieved of their ignorance by a simple answer; instead they glimpse a complicated thought process and further questioning which will make them feel increasingly stupid.

Strolling in the department stores along the Boulevard Haussmann, vaguely looking for clothes. I feel numbed, visited by a series of fantasies which flare up and fade—a Chacock sweater, a Carroll cardigan, a demure pleated dress; images of me file by, in blue, in red, with a V-neck, continually forming and drifting apart. I feel I am being assaulted by shapes and colors, torn apart by these bright things, scores of them, which we wrap around our body.

When I emerge on to the dark, damp sidewalk I realize that in fact I didn't need a jersey, or a dress, or anything.

On the marketplace in Les Linandes, two children are playing at being airplanes, their arms outstretched. One of them shouts excitedly: "It goes up in the air!" Then, in a different voice, resigned, as if faced with some terrible fatality, he adds: "And crashes." He takes pleasure in repeating the axiom several times, faster and faster, running round in circles.

A man is questioning a young woman on the train heading toward Paris: "How many hours a week do you work?" "What time do you start work?" "Can you choose when you take your vacation?" We all need to assess the advantages and constraints of a profession, the material side of life. Not out of harmless curiosity, or to make polite conversation, but to learn about other people's lives so that we can learn about our own life or the life we might have chosen.

I caught sight of the young man who used to collect the shopping carts at Franprix last year. He was in that very supermarket, shopping with a woman. He was wearing a jacket over a long sweater, with bright chains hanging from his pants. The woman asked him loudly, pointing to the "Président" Camembert cheeses: "Shall we get a 'Président'?" He replied: "Do you think they'll let us take him home?" The woman did not laugh but continued to peer at the shelves. He was the same man I had seen lean-ing against the wall in the parking lot, except that now he looked free and happy, with his punk symbols hanging down his side, and a woman. I noticed they had no shopping cart.

The two women—probably the manager and an employee—were chatting beside the cash register while customers were looking around for the hardware articles they needed. "She can't understand why he gets home late; she's an academic, it's different from trade. Of course she can't understand why her husband works such long hours. She has no idea what it's like to be in trade.

—That's quite true!" the manager exclaims, repeating loudly; "That is perfectly true!" insisting on the word *true*, which in this case was not opposed to *false*, it signified a wonderful discovery, an idea which, to her astonishment, had never occurred to the manager of the hardware store, although it had occurred quite naturally to her employee.

A woman's voice, through the loud speaker, explains the history of May Day. Then it announces that today there's a special on aperitifs and hi-fi equipment. The hypermarket may want to enlighten customers and show that it can play an educational role, or else it's a commercial ploy to lessen the onslaught of advertising. In a few years from now, in the middle of hypermarkets, we shall probably see cinema screens, promotional lectures on painting or literature, maybe even lessons on computers. A sort of peep-show corner.

Every evening, a radio station compares two songs, a recent hit and one released earlier, sometimes only one year before. Listeners call in to say which song they prefer. Most of them are young; many are girls. The emcee then picks a listener "at random," or so he says, and asks them to guess which song is the most popular. The winning song is invariably the most recent one.

Yesterday, the shampoo girl in the hairdresser's salon remarked: "Women's fashion is so much more attractive nowadays. People had terrible taste ten years ago."

Her comments reflect the perfect correspondence that exists between the younger generation and their epoch, and the belief that what has "just come out" is always better. Otherwise, it would mean having no faith in oneself, let alone in the future.

A woman was complaining angrily to the post office clerk about a mistake in the delivery of her mail. Faced with so much resentment, the clerk was standing her ground, refusing to investigate the matter and replying in an aggressive manner. It's only natural to express grievances by adopting the same emotional mood as the one aroused by those very grievances. For instance, something sad is related in a sad voice, something happy in a happy voice, and so on. Improvised acting, equating form with content. To disassociate the exposition of a problem from the anxiety caused by that problem is something requiring both concentration and detachment, as well as the understanding that the person opposite you does not share your feelings; all they can perceive is your hostile attitude, which they see as a personal affront. If, on the other hand, you choose to be polite—an insincere attitude, expressing neither kindness nor interest in the clerk—your complaint will be given immediate attention.

Two children whose parents had allowed them to starve to death were mentioned on the news. The radio and television commentators were surprised that the doctor had failed to intervene. Nobody thought of saying, or wanted to say, that, quite unintentionally, the doctor had not examined these children, born to a Fourth World couple, as attentively as he examined children coming from a family of middle-class executives. He probably thought it normal for the little ones to be underfed and mentally retarded because of their background. He let things take their course and, sure enough, the parents, plagued by illiteracy, poverty and eight young kids, behaved as was to be expected, showing insensitivity and indifference toward the extra mouths to feed. It's the natural course of society—on the side of the parents, on the side of the doctor.

A shopping cart on its side, a long way from the mall, like a toy forgotten in the grass.

At the height of August, a little old woman, fresh and rosy-cheeked, with white ankle socks and a straw hat, is standing motionless in the middle of the Trois-Fontaines shopping center; she looks lost. She is surrounded by a store selling sportswear, the jeweler La Baguerie and Nicolas, the wine merchant.

In the RER, somewhere behind me, right at the back, a drunken man keeps repeating in a loud voice: "I got nothing to be afraid of. When you have a clear conscience, you got no reason to be afraid." Then: "I voted for Le Pen. A guy like Le Pen, he's for the Arabs, the ones who work. The ones who cheat, out!" All the passengers stare down at their newspaper or look out of the window. When I got off at Nanterre, I caught sight of the man—in his fifties, sporting a sailor's cap.

In the Leclerc hypermarket, out shopping, I catch the strains of *Voyage*. I wonder if the emotion and the pleasure I experience, as well as the feeling of panic that the song will end, have anything to do with the violent impression left by certain books, such as *Le Bel Été* by Pavese, or Faulkner's *Sanctuary*. The feelings aroused by the song of Desireless are intense, almost painful, leading to a form of frustration which does not fade with repetition (in the past I would listen to a record three, five, ten times running, waiting for something that never happened). A book offers more *deliverance*, more escape, more fulfillment of desire. In songs one remains locked in desire. (The lyrics are not that important, only the melody matters; so I understood nothing of what the Platters or the Beatles were saying.) There are no places, no scenes, no characters, only oneself and one's longing. Yet the very starkness and paucity of music allow me to recall a whole episode of my life and the girl I used to be when I listen to *I'm Just Another Dancing Partner* thirty years later. Whereas the beauty and fullness of *Le Bel Été* and *A la Recherche du Temps Perdu*, which I have reread two or three times, can never give me back my life.

The hairdresser is overexcited, addressing the salon at large when in fact she is speaking to another hairdresser who is doing a shampoo and set next to her. "I noticed right away. I said to her, you've got lice, and she answers, no I haven't, how dare you. But Madame, I say, I can tell lice when I see them! I refused to do her hair. You know, she got real mad, she started yelling at me!" The hairdresser continues co comment on the incident frenziedly, in a loud voice, as if she wants the greatest number of people to know about this act of insolence—a woman with lice daring to come to *her* salon—thus cleansing herself of the personal affront she had endured on discovering the little beasts.

The little girl on the train to Paris—she and her mother had got on at Achères-Ville—had sunglasses in the shape of two hearts and a small apple-green basket of plaited plastic. She was three, maybe four years old and was not smiling, clasping her basket to her chest, her head nice and straight behind the sunglasses. Sheer happiness at displaying the first signs of "ladyhood," at finally possessing the things one craved.

On a sunny day like today, the seams of buildings lacerate the sky, the glass surfaces radiate light. I have lived in the New Town for twelve years, yet I still don't know what it looks like. I am unable to describe it, not knowing where it begins or ends; I always drive through it. I can only write down, "I went to the Leclerc hypermarket (or to the Trois-Fontaines shopping mall, to the Franprix in Les Linandes, etc.), I turned back on to the freeway, the sky was purple beyond the Marcouville high-rise apartments (or on the 3M Minnesota façade)." No description, no story either. Just moments in time, chance meetings. Ethnowriting.

One of the salesgirls from the perfume store in the Trois-Fontaines shopping mall, the one who has been there the longest—three years already—is at least six months pregnant. Swollen features; slow-footed, forever smiling. "This mascara dries up quickly"; she laughs at the remark. Then asks: "How quickly?—After four months." She throws back her head and bursts into peals of laughter: "Well, that's logical!" She is still laughing as I leave the perfume store—that dizzy state peculiar to pregnant women in which they find the slightest thing amusing.

The number one hit in the Top 50 says: "Hey, you guys, why not stop by for a drink; we got red wine, we got white wine, we got salami—and good old Emile has gotten out his accordion." My first impression: "How could people who like that sort of music ever enjoy Mozart?" Today I thought the melody was light-hearted; it felt like a Sunday: the sun is out, our buddies will be here any moment. This song, which says "the women came, locked away the *pernod* and shouted louder than us," reflects the daily life of a great many people; it only seems shocking to those who haven't seen women snatch bottles away from the table, barking: "You've had enough." Such people would welcome a song that described, or even denounced, the *pernod*-salami lifestyle but a song that exalts the virtues of working-class conviviality would be seen as an offense.

On the walls of a lecture hall where a professor is explaining Proust, at Nanterre University:
Unrestricted pleasure
Free sexuality
Free love
Student you're sleeping
You're wasting your life
We must achieve economic equality

At Les Comptoirs de la Tour d'Argent, on the Quai de la Tournelle—a store attached to the famous restaurant—you cannot just walk in, you have to ring first. From the outside, you can see a table laid for two, flowers, and a couple eating. As soon as you walk through the door, you realize they are wax figures. A man is buying a pair of "La Tour d'Argent" slippers—black, embroidered with pink flowers. He wants to know if he can try them on. He sits down near the mannequins, surrounded by fine glassware and vintage bottles. There are very few items on show—all are expensive and all are signed. I feel I am in a store selling funerary objects. The *foie gras* sold here is contained in small urns of white china.

After Christmas, Marguerite Duras and Jean-Luc Godard had a "talk" on television. In other words, a conversation between two artists, normally conducted in private, at home or at a café table, is shown to other people. They speak freely, as if there were no cameras, no technicians bustling about the living-room (the superior way of being "natural"). Duras says to Godard: "You've got a problem with writing. That's your handicap." He says yes, no. What they actually say is of no consequence; what does matter is that a conversation between artists or intellectuals is made available to the rest of society. A perfect model of conversation.

Godard and Duras command respect. Anything vaguely cultural commands respect. There was no respect for Bourvil or Fernandel when they were alive, nor for the late comedian Coluche. Death too can be a passport to culture.

      In Paris, on New Year's Eve, on the streets, in subway and RER stations, and outside the department stores on the Boulevard Haussmann, all the beggars, both young and old, were chanting "Happy New Year! Happy New Year!" The Havre-Caumartin station echoed with a terrible rumbling, loud and menacing. One wondered if suddenly they were going to pick themselves off the ground, all together, and assault the passers-by laden with shopping bags and presents, claiming their due.

1988

"Go home!" the man tells his dog; it slinks away, submissive, guilty. The same expression used throughout history for children, women and dogs.

Saint-Lazare station, on a Saturday: a couple are waiting in line for a taxi. She looks lost and leans on him for support. He keeps repeating: "You'll see when I'm dead." Then: "I want to be burned, you know, I want to be burned from head to toe. I don't want to go into that thing. It's horrible, that thing." He clutches her to his chest; she is panicked.

I am visited by people and their lives—like a whore.

At the drugstore, a woman buys medicine for her husband: "After he's swallowed all that, he doesn't feel like eating." Then she mentions that he refuses to "keep warm" and take it easy, adding with a laugh, "If he was a child, he'd get his face slapped!" Words handed down from one generation to the next, missing from newspapers and books, ignored by schools, belonging to populist culture (originally my own, which is why I immediately identify it).

No one talks on the crowded seven o' clock morning train to Paris, except maybe a few drowsy passengers. In a sleepy voice, one woman tells the woman opposite her about the dead fish she found in her aquarium: "I stirred the water in the tank but it didn't move. Then, when I saw it float to the surface, I said to myself, 'Oh well, that's it'." A little later, recalling the same incident, she repeats, "so I said to myself, 'Oh well, that's it'." While she is speaking, another woman near the window is listening to her, staring at her intently. The lights were yellow; people were suffocating in their winter coats. The windows of the train were covered in steam.

At the Chambre des Députés subway station, the "Dé" has been scratched away: Chambre des putes (Chamber of whores). A sign of Antiparliamentarism. The current belief is that this inevitably leads to fascism. But the person who erased the "Dé" may have wanted simply to amuse himself and other people. Can one disassociate the immediate and personal implications of someone's act from its possible future implications and consequences?

A group of youngsters hanging out at the railroad station in the New Town, near the escalator. A single girl surrounded by boys. As I walk by, she says jauntily: "You didn't tell your buddies I was two and a half months pregnant by you, did you?" Seconds later, the sound of laughter. As if the girl were in a desert swept by the wind.

These days, a commercial can be heard on almost all radio stations—a man's voice, suave, with soft music in the background: "Welcome to the world of RHÔNE-POULENC, a world open to challenge" and so on.

In the subway car, a man begs for a coin or a meal ticket: "I'm jobless." He holds out his hand in vain. As he gets off at

Concorde, he mutters to himself: "I really haven't got much money."

Waiting in line at the Franprix check-out, an Asian woman was carrying the satchel of her little boy, just out of school and playing beside her.

A platform at the RER station next to Nanterre University, on a Saturday, one evening in May. Men and women aged between thirty and sixty, all carrying paper bags bearing the inscription "La Reine Pédauque," containing three liters of wine. The sound of continual laughter. The women, more talkative, are discussing what a great time they had (somewhere in Normandy, it would seem). There is more laughter as they remember the times when they laughed. Recalling the circumstances in which the events that prompted the laughter took place, laughing even louder because now it's all over. (Similarly, remembering all the motions of lovemaking heightens the pleasure of fantasy. Literature too allows us to relive pleasure and pain.) They mention visiting a "drugstore," maybe a store selling "natural produce." One of the women remarks: "This guy, he says to me, do you have a dog? If his shit comes out white, you must keep the turds."

She doubles up with laughter and repeats: "If his shit comes out white!"

They form a group and all know one another, as if they belonged to the same firm; so they speak out loud when they mention the other passengers, lonely and excluded: "Look, the lady has left her seat, the train must be due in." One man said: "We could have gotten off at Poissy, it would have brought us closer to home," and, when someone suggests going to a pancake restaurant to round off the evening, "We've had too much to eat, a pancake would be a waste!" Another woman exclaims: "Can that guy put it away!" I am surprised to hear these words and expressions so typical of my childhood days. My reaction confirms a well-known truth: we believe, because we stop using them, that certain words have disappeared, or that poverty has ceased to exist now that we earn a living. Strangely enough, there exists another truth, the exact opposite: when we go back to a town we left a long time ago, we imagine that the people there will still be the same, unchanged. Both laws rely on the same misconception of reality, the only reference being oneself: in the first case, we imagine everyone else has lived our life, while in the second, we long to recapture our past identity through people who are frozen in time, whose features are the same as when we last saw them.

After tomorrow, Saint-Lazare station will no longer be the gateway into Paris for me and the other residents of the New Town. We shall approach the city on the RER, stopping at the underground stations of Charles-de-Gaulle, Auber, Les Halles, etc. This morning I gazed around at the hall, the glass roof and the birds flitting underneath. Nine years of my life will come to an end because the train route between Cergy and Paris has been altered. From now on there will be the days of the Cergy-Saint-Lazare train and the days of the RER A line.

At Hédiard, in the smart, fashionable area of the New Town, a black woman wearing a *boubou* walked into the store. Immediately, the manager's gaze became razor sharp, relentlessly pursuing this new client, whom one suspects has come to the wrong store, who doesn't realize she is out of place.

For the first time I took the direct RER line linking Cergy to Paris. I shall no longer see the train drawing in between the blackened walls of Saint-Lazare station, the sun on the façades overhanging the exposed rails, the signs in the Rue de Rome—"Hôtel Champlain," "Ecole supérieure de secrétariat"—the crowds massing on to the platforms. This morning it

all became memory: the evening wait in front of train sched-
ules, the announcements made through loud speakers, the
twinkling blue lights of the trains at night, people running all
over the place, trying to meet (how can anyone possibly meet
at an RER station?). Now you enter Paris along underground
tunnels, amid artificial lights, not knowing where you are.

Yet there was beauty in the huge twin escalators at Charles-
de-Gaulle, in the silence too. Then, the approaching rumble of
an orchestra; women lingering at a stand selling jewelry. It was
eight o' clock in the morning.

I ask the young girl who is doing my hair: "Do
you enjoy reading?" She replies: "Oh! I don't mind reading
but I haven't got time." ("I don't mind" washing the dishes,
cooking, being on my feet all day—the expression is used to
indicate that one is willing to do certain chores. It seems that
reading is one of them.)

A survey was published in the newspaper. It
revealed the strong impact of material symbols: no one has
qualms about insulting God yet very few people would agree

to spit on a crucifix (even fewer would consider using it as a dildo). People consent to desert but not to trample their country's flag. These objects, which we were taught to respect when we were small, have acquired a sacred dimension and considerable power; they can be seen and touched, and therefore their abuse is considered to be an immediate and visible attack on the world. Thoughts and words do not have as strong an influence as physical action. It is easy for people to wish their enemy ill-luck but very few would actually consider getting a doll and sticking pins into it in order to visualize and carry out their evil intentions. Not because they scorn superstition but simply because they recoil at committing an act whose finality is transgression for its own sake.

A new tramp can be seen begging on the RER between Cergy and Paris. His technique is based on confession: "I'm not a thief or a murderer, I'm a tramp!" and "Give me some money so that I can buy myself some food and something to drink!" (To say "I'm out of a job" immediately arouses feelings of suspicion and anger—why doesn't he look for one, etc.) He announces: "I'm coming your way now, please give me a few coins, folding money is welcome too." People laugh, they appreciate his sense of humor. He receives a lot of money; to the passengers who give something he bawls, "Have a nice day!" and to the passengers who give nothing, "Have a lousy day!" Those who laugh are on his side. As he leaves the car, he yells: "Well, folks, see you tomorrow." All the people roar with laughter. His approach is excellent in that it respects the social hierarchy: I'm a tramp, I drink and I don't work—quite the opposite of you. He does not denounce social values, he reaffirms them. A buffoon, he is there to keep his traveling audience at a fair distance from the social reality, poverty and alcoholism, represented by himself. A role he performs instinctively, and with great talent.

I got off the subway at Poissonnière and walked up the Rue La Fayette until I reached the Eglise Saint-Vincent-de-Paul. The church is approached by a flight of steps. A girl was sunbathing, sitting on the stone, writing a letter. A couple was kissing. I felt I was in Rome, climbing up the flower-decked steps of the Trinità dei Monti, toward the sun. Then I turned into the Boulevard Magenta, looking for number 106, Hôtel de Suède, which used to be called the Sphinx Hôtel. The façade was sheathed in a tarpaulin; the whole of the interior was being demolished. One of the workers leaned out of a window; he looked at me with amusement and said something to the others. I was standing motionless on the opposite sidewalk, gazing up at the hotel (which they may be converting into private apartments). He thought I was returning to a place that held memories for me, as a lover or a whore. In fact I am reliving the memories of another woman, Nadja, the Nadja associated with André Breton, who lived in this hotel around 1927. Displayed in the window where I was standing were outmoded pairs of shoes, of a single color, black, and slippers, also black. It looked like a store for mourning shoes or ecclesiastical footwear. I continued down the Boulevard Magenta and turned into a small alleyway, the Ruelle de la Ferme-Saint-Lazare; it was deserted. A man was sitting on his doorstep. Bloody remains soiled the cobblestones. Then I turned back into the Rue La Fayette and walked on until I got to the café "La Nouvelle France," with its old-fashioned curtains. Framed in the entrance, a boy was waving to an Eurasian girl on the other side of the street. I continued to follow in Nadja's footsteps in the sort of daze that intensifies all one's emotions.

At Cluny, a tall, light-haired boy, with a red parka and clean beige trousers, is crouching against the wall of the subway corridor, his head bent forward, his knees pressing into his stomach. He has a knapsack beside him and a notice in front of him. I didn't read it. All the time I was walking toward the platform, I kept wanting to go back to read the notice and give him some money. Then, at one point, it became impossible for me to retrace my steps. I had the impression that I had just seen one of my own sons begging for money.

There were plenty of people on the RER at six o' clock that evening. A woman sitting near the window kept glancing at the aisle, where passengers were crowding in. Wherever her gaze settled, there were only women to be seen. She was dark, smooth, with a gray jacket and striped pants; a black handbag protruded from her document case. On her slender hands—a wedding ring. The woman she was eyeing was not the heavily made-up blonde who resembled a model but a short, plump brunette in a beige skirt and matching blouse. Realizing she was being watched, the small, rounded passenger averted her eyes, then pulled in her stomach. Her white bra was showing through her blouse. She composed her features into a vague, permanent smile. The other woman continued to stare at her unblinkingly. The small brunette glanced at me with amusement, as if she wanted to draw me into the seduction scene that was being played out to her. She was delighted at having been chosen, be it without her consent. I suddenly remembered the school playground, where we used to giggle with pleasure and embarrassment, hand covering mouth, exchanging glances, because Geneviève C showed us her vulva. That was in grade school, before the days of boys.

F and her friend have taken portraits of writers in the photographic studio they recently opened in the Rue du Chemin-Vert. Now, when they are discussing one of them, they use their first name, in the manner of "Johnny's" (Halliday) groupies, although they both despise the latter, "Yves' book is selling well, we're very happy for him." They believe, or would like others to believe, that they share a certain intimacy with the author. They also say "Virginia" instead of Virginia Woolf but not "Marcel" (Proust) or "Louis-Ferdinand" (Céline).

This morning, while I was out walking my bitch, who is in heat, I met the little old lady who keeps her mongrel on a leash—a lively dog, on the alert as soon as he gets a whiff of us. We exchanged greetings. I am beginning to reach the age when I say hello to the old women I meet in my neighborhood, anticipating the moment in life when I shall be one of them. When I was twenty I didn't notice them; they would be dead before my face had wrinkles.

Sitting at Les Halles, hemmed in between two bands performing on the station platform. A cacophony in which one is slowly drained.

A rhetorical scene is being played out at the Charles-de-Gaulle-Étoile station, at half past nine at night. A young drunkard calls out to a man in his forties who is sitting on the platform—a dropout, but not quite a tramp, still this side of respectability: "Fuck you!" Then, louder: "Fuck you! I said fuck you!" The older man: "Why are you so aggressive? Be polite when you speak to me." During the ensuing conversation, the guy who denies being a tramp explains to the younger man that they cannot communicate because of the brash, hostile tone used by the latter. "You come up and say to me, 'fuck you,' now I know what to fuck means, and I can't answer you. If you'd spoken politely and calmly, we could have had something to say to each other but with your attitude, no way. I can't answer you, I don't want to." The young man resumes his aggressive approach, while the other continues to lay down the rules of proper conversation in a "normal" world, from which he has already been excluded materially, but whose traditions he wishes to maintain, like ruined aristocrats who persist in kissing ladies' hands. However, the younger tramp is no fool; he realizes that by agreeing to speak to him—be it about the art of conversation—the hobo who refuses to see himself as such is clearly on the way there. All the passengers on the platform hide behind their newspaper or look the other way.

I realize that there are two ways of dealing with real facts. One can either relate them in detail, exposing their stark, immediate nature, outside of any narrative form, or else save them for future reference, "making use" of them by incorporating them into an ensemble (a novel, for instance). Fragments of writing, like the ones in this book, arouse in me a feeling of frustration. I need to become involved in a lengthy, structured process (unaffected by chance events and meetings). Yet at the same time I have this need to record scenes glimpsed on the RER, and people's words and gestures simply *for their own sake*, without any ulterior motive.

On the walls of the railroad station in Cergy, after the October riots, one could read: ALGERIA I LOVE YOU, with a blood-red flower between "Algeria" and "I."

1989

Throughout the day, the old painter who is restoring the façade has been scolding his young apprentice, putting him down: "Stop trying to be a smart-ass," or "Don't put your hands there! God, you're dumb! You know, you're real dumb, but it's not your fault, you were born that way." The apprentice resumes his cheerful singing; the old man looks contented. Words of no consequence, ritualistic, almost affectionate. Reminiscent of old times.

The station at Saint-Lazare is no longer part of my life; all I can see and hear now are the RER stations, the silence at Auber, the muffled, uniformly sad music coming from "Tube" (an internal TV network set up by the Paris Transport System), the intermingling bands at Les Halles, the noiseless approach of the train cars, the heat, the lights. The twenty-first century succeeding the nineteenth century of Saint-Lazare station.

A few weeks ago a new "begging technique" appeared: "Gimme a couple of francs so that I can go get drunk." He's a young man, with a ring through one ear. Cynicism has replaced the demand for pity. There are no limits to man's creativity.

I would love to remember *when* the first beggar appeared at the entrance to the Trois-Fontaines shopping mall, in the New Town: was it last summer (1989)?

A young girl on the RER is unwrapping the things she has bought: a blouse and a pair of earrings. She contemplates them and touches them lovingly. It's a common enough scene: happiness at possessing something beautiful, at seeing one's longing for beauty satisfied. Our relationship to things is so moving.

At the bus stop in front of the Cergy-Préfecture station, a woman is violently reprimanding her teenage daughter: "I won't always be here! One day you'll have to manage on your own!"

I can still hear my father or mother saying: "We won't

always be here!" with that particular intonation they had. I can still recall the sudden seriousness of their features. At the time the sentence was meaningless since they were both there beside me. It was just a vague threat used for blackmailing me into working hard, taking care of my belongings, and so on. When I think about that sentence today, it still doesn't mean anything. It was a threat proffered by living people; now both of them are dead. "You'll see when we're gone!" Only the reality of this sentence remains—absurd, fearful, mouthed by others.

Florence. The restroom in the Palazzo Vecchio, ladies' side. A small notice: 200 lira. A man in his sixties is responsible for the efficient running and cleanliness of the place, comprising four or five cubicles. Women wait in line at the entrance. The custodian of the latrines bustles about, inspecting the premises after each visit, looking serious. A young man of around twenty leaves one of the toilets, wiping his hands on a paper tissue, under the glare of the women and their mute questions, "what's he doing in here, in the ladies' restroom"—the handwashing arouses suspicion—"has he been jerking off?" The attendant rushes into the lavatory the boy has just left and makes a big show of washing down the floor with a mop, noisily flushing the toilet, and cleaning the bowl and sink, then signals to a woman that now she can go in. His disapproval at seeing the premises sullied is conveyed by this fastidious display of cleanliness and each woman feels she must leave the place as spotless as she found it: indeed, after each visit, the attendant gives a cursory glance, then nods to the woman next in line. Clearly, the man derives pleasure from catering to the satisfaction of women's bodily needs. He is a paid satyr at the head of a cosmopolitan harem, forever renewed. His lasciviousness is redeemed by the excellency of his standards in matters of hygiene and by his quest for pristine white tiles, for perfection.

The posters for the relief agency "Secours Catholique" read UNLEASH YOUR EMOTIONS. It shows poor people, in other words, people bearing the stigmata of poverty such as it is seen by the ruling class. Nobody asked these poor people what they thought of this vision of slumped bodies, frayed clothes and dazed expressions.

An advertisement published in the computer mag *L'Ordinateur Individuel*. On the righthand page, three men and a woman. Two of the men in suits, the woman in a black dress, real sexy. The third man's face is slightly out of focus; he is wearing corduroy trousers, a red sweater, and looks vaguely bohemian. Under these silhouettes, one can read; WE

ARE GOING TO TELL YOU WHY WE MADE IT. The same characters appear on the following page. The first one says: "I made it because I read *L'Ordinateur Individuel* and because my father is CEO." The next two characters display the same cynical sense of humor. The fourth person, the man in the red sweater, *has disappeared*. The man whose failure was dictated by his old-fashioned clothes and laid-back attitude (the others were upright and energetic) has been obliterated from the landscape of success: annihilated, NIL. This word was introduced under the liberalism of the eighties. It offers a contemporary definition of the subman. (In French, the adjective *nul*, originally meaning non-existent, became a synonym of worthless or useless.)

At Super-Discount, a young cashier, maybe a temp, is laughing with some people she knows, two girls standing beside her. The customers waiting in line are visibly annoyed: it's quite clear she doesn't give a damn about us, she's just ringing up the items, period. People resent her openness.

In a subway car, a boy and a girl argue and stroke each other, alternately, as if they were alone in the world.

But they know that's not true: every now and then they stare insolently at the other passengers. My heart sinks. I tell myself that writing is this for me.

1990

On a Friday evening, a couple in their late for-
ties buy meat for the whole week. One after the other, alternately, they reel off their requests: "a couple of pork chops, a piece
of beef shin, with the bone? yes, sure," occasionally consulting
each other, "what about some potato chips?" The owner and
his young assistant exchange pleasantries with the couple. The
more they buy, the more excited they get. "The guinea-fowl I've
put in is smaller than the chicken, okay?—No problem, we'll
line them up side by side and whichever one eats the other will
be the winner!" The man laughs as he turns round to face the
other customers. The scene is indecent. It's impossible to say if
their contentment comes from flaunting their material wealth
or their convivial nature, their appetite for food, echoing their
sexual appetite, which it may have come to replace. (It's easy

to imagine them sitting opposite each other, eating in silence, evening after evening until they die.)

On the outskirts of Nanterre, a temporary housing development was built for the immigrant population in the sixties. Now all that remain are the concrete slabs marking the foundations of each house. For twenty years, people lived here, children too. From the train you could see them playing in the mud. In 1990 many of the passengers traveling on the A line of the RER are unaware of the significance of these slabs, which remind one of tombstones and where the grass still only grows back in patches.

The "authoress," a petite redhead with curls, is standing against the wall inside a basement bookstore near the Pompidou Center. Beside her, her publisher presents her work and praises her courage. Now it's her turn to speak, wrapped in a purple shawl, bracelets high up her arm, rings adorning her slender fingers. A vivacious woman. "To write is to slip into decline," she muses, luxuriating in the role of an accursed writer, a victim of social abandon. The people standing in a half-circle around her, holding glasses of country wine, gravely nod in agreement. Naturally, they feel no compassion, knowing full well that her decline is a fake (true deprivation cannot be expressed in words and is never a deliberate choice) and that they too would like to "slip into decline," in other words, to write. The authoress is well aware that they envy her. In the minds of those present, the truth is in the right place.

1991

The Rue des Saints-Pères, on a bitter February evening. The lingerie store Sabbia Rosa: everywhere you look—silk in soft, candy hues, reminiscent of the sun rising above the Indian Ocean or the blossom in Claude Monet's garden. No eroticism, or maybe just a distant hint; instead beauty, fragility and airiness (the contents of the whole store could easily fit into a trunk). I thought: "I understand why people prostitute themselves to own such things." (One cannot call them by their technical names: panties, brassieres, etc.) Wanting to have some of this beauty on one's skin is as legitimate as wanting to breathe fresh air. These "undies," separated from the flesh, conjure up an image of perfect nudity. The undies displayed here will never be seen again, except by the man for whom they were chosen. They are not so much futile as sacred. Men should wear silk lingerie so that we can enjoy the pleasure of seeing and touching these soft, delicate fabrics on their skin.

At the Sorbonne, a notice on the main glass door of the library informs the public that, until 1st October, the entrance to the library is through staircase B, on the third floor. You have to go back out into the courtyard and take the staircase they mention. On the third floor, you walk successively through two small, heavy doors that slam shut and into a corridor constricted by rows of books piled up to the ceiling. There is a desk where a woman checks your membership card and gives you a number as well as a green form for taking out books. An arrow points toward the reading room. You cross the cataloguing room and continue along corridors that branch off in several directions. The walls are lined with books closed in behind wire netting. All the covers have taken on the same, indefinite color; it's impossible to read the titles, except maybe from close up. I feel I am walking past one big dusty book. At the end of the corridor, the reading room was shrouded in silence. I filled in the green form supplied by the lending library. I was given only one book; opposite the titles of the other two, someone had written "not available." I retraced my steps along the corridor with wire netting. In sixty years' time, everything that I have seen, loved and enjoyed may have disappeared, replaced by a stack of printed pages, to be consulted only for some obscure thesis.

On Sunday morning, the radio station RTL broadcasts *Your Choice*, a program relying on a proven formula: one attracts a large number of listeners by asking them to vote against or in favor of a particular song, which one then plays, and by leading them to believe they can win a certain sum of money. There is no connection between voting yes or no and winning the money. After five songs, the emcee calls somebody at random, listed in the phone book, and asks them to tell him how much money there is in the kitty, referred to as the "trunk." All you need to do to pocket the money is tune in and memorize a figure.

In a solemn voice, the emcee declares there are 27,219 francs in the "trunk." Then: "Watch out, now I'm going to call one of our listeners . . ." You can hear the phone ringing, the receiver being picked up. A faint, uncertain voice answers: "Hello, who's calling?—Julien Lepers, from RTL. Is that Madame Lefebvre?—No, I'm Jérémie . . ." The emcee says with authority: "Can you go and fetch your mummy or daddy?—My daddy's in the garden and my mummy's busy but I don't know where . . ." The emcee insists:

"But surely you can go and tell them there's someone's on the phone?" The child appears to hesitate, then makes up his mind. There's a pause. The emcee grows impatient and announces the songs he is going to play; the singer is Umberto Tozzi. Suddenly, a woman's voice inquires: "Hello?" The emcee, jovially: "Madame Lefebvre? This is Julien Lepers, from RTL, calling you about the 'trunk'." The woman utters a short scream: "Oh! Damn . . .

—You weren't listening to RTL.

—I listen to you every week!

—But you weren't listening this morning!

—No, but I usually do on Saturday and Sunday!

—But not this morning!

—You know, we had some friends round last night and . . . my little boy isn't feeling . . .

—What a pity."

The woman wants to be forgiven for her failing. So many dreams offered and snatched back at the same time.

"Promise me you'll listen to RTL?

—Oh! Yes! I promise!"

The telephone conversation ends. The emcee gives the title of the next song and the amount of money now contained in the "trunk," which increases with each loser.

At the Charles-de-Gaulle-Étoile station, a man in his thirties gets into a subway car and sits down on a folding seat. He's wearing a gray two-piece suit; there's nothing special about him, except maybe his tennis shoes, which look slightly out of place. Suddenly he leans forward and rolls one trouser leg up to his knee. You can see the alabaster skin bristling with hairs. He pulls up his sock with both hands, gives it a tug, then rolls down the trouser leg. He does the same thing with the other sock.

Later on, he stands up, leans against the wall, undoes his jacket and lifts his tee-shirt. He scrutinizes his stomach for some time, then pulls down his tee-shirt. Clearly, his actions are not intended to provoke; they are the ultimate manifestation of loneliness—true loneliness—in the midst of the crowd. Beside him, there's a plastic bag, the trademark of the homeless. When someone loses their home and their job, how long does it take before the presence of other people no longer prevents them from doing perfectly normal things which, in public, are considered to be unacceptable? When do they start to drop the "good manners" they were once taught at school and at home, over the dining-room table, when they used to fall asleep dreaming of the big bright future? He got off at Auber.

"In the museum of Basel there's a painting by . . ." (Instead of Basel, one could have said Amsterdam or

85

Florence or any other big city.) The opening of a sentence, anonymous, unremarkable, commonly heard or read, immediately implying that one belongs to a certain world. A world familiar with painting, of course, but also a world of open-minded, discriminating travelers, a world comfortable enough for a painting to take up space in one's life and memory. A world poles apart from Saturday shopping expeditions with the kids, and crowded campsites in August.

First it is a fleeting impression, a light touch against my hip, or maybe my back, as I climb the escalator leading to the exit of the Havre-Caumartin station. Someone is standing right behind me. As I reach the top of the escalator, the feeling grows stronger, although I can't quite define it. My handbag is slung over my shoulder; I bring it back in front of me. It is wide open: the fastener has been undone, the flap thrown back. But nothing is missing. I turn round angrily. He's a young boy in an overcoat, calmly smoking a cigarette. I exclaim: "What the hell d'you thing you're doing?" He smiles, says "Excuse me, Madame" and, alighting from the escalator, saunters off in the opposite direction.

I walk along the Boulevard Haussmann, then between the counters of the Printemps department store, distracted, incapable of paying attention to the fashion accessories on display. I feel uneasy; out of all the women carrying handbags, I had to be chosen against my will to feature in some cheap pickpocket scenario. It's nothing more than a vague feeling of humiliation, made worse by the boy's nonchalant attitude and his calm apology, implying that his activities are only a game. There's an element of risk: sometimes you win—only he could say how often—and sometimes you lose, in which case you must accept defeat. The real humiliation, however, was that so much confidence, expertise and longing was channelled toward my handbag, and not my body.

1992

Tonight, at Les Halles, just as the RER doors were about to snap shut, two tramps entered noisily and sat down on opposite seats. Two shaggy, unkempt men in tattered clothes. The younger of the two, aged between thirty and forty, lays an empty bottle down on the floor and opens *Libération*. The other one, around fifty, maybe younger, starts to bawl the French national anthem. He spits into a rag and says: "Who cares about the army? Look at that gob of spittle, you won't see another one like that, not even in the army." Then, trying to engage his companion in conversation, he asks: "Why d'you look like a fag?" The other one ignores the trite insult, delivered with friendly intent, and exclaims: "You've got the Serbs! You've got the Croats! It's a good thing we got newspapers, otherwise I'd be a real ignoramus." He rustles the paper. "See that? Some people make it to Gabon and we only end up in Sartrouville." A short silence. "It's just not fair." The older man echoes his thoughts: "It's just not fair." Then: "I want to go back into my egg, it was nice and cosy."

The man reading *Libération* goes on muttering "it's just not fair," while taking an interest in this imaginary subject: "Did you have a shell over your head?

—No, it was skin. I may not be a gynecologist, but I'm not a moron!

—I don't want to leave! It's a great squat—real warm!

—I wanted to stay so badly my mom had to have a Caesarian.

—At the time, they used chainsaws to do Caesarians.

—She suffered a lot. That's why she never acknowledged me.

—Mine didn't either."

This verbal sparring, wavering between violence and self-pity, is performed with ostentation for the benefit of the twenty odd passengers traveling in the RER car. But, contrary to a real theater, members of the audience here avoid looking at the actors and affect not to hear their performance. Embarrassed to see real life making a spectacle of itself, and not the opposite.

The two men get off at Sartrouville. They leave behind the empty bottle, which rolls under the seats.

I must have dozed off on the express train somewhere after the last stop. (Angoulême station, around eight o' clock at night: deserted platforms—in the poorly-lit entrance there's a man with a dog, peering at a bulletin board—it feels like a night train stopping at a town where everyone is sound asleep.) I pull the curtain to one side. On the stretch of houses, a huge luminous sign for the Mammoth hypermarket, then, further along, one for Miami (a night club or maybe a shopping mall?). I am flooded with relief as I recognize the signs belonging to the outskirts of Paris. I experience the same feeling when, approaching the Gennevilliers viaduct along highway A 15, I suddenly discover a sweeping panorama of factories, buildings and pre-war suburban houses, set against the backdrop of Paris and La Défense.

On the RER a young man, tall, with sturdy legs and thick lips, occupies a seat giving on to the aisle. Across the way, there's a woman with a two or three-year-old boy on her lap; he is looking all around, sort of stunned, his eyes filled with wonder. Then he asks "how do they close the doors." It's probably the first time he has been on the RER. Both of them, the young man and the little boy, take me back to moments in my life. First, to the year when I took my *baccalauréat,* in May, when D, a tall boy with big lips like the guy sitting over there, used to wait for me after high school, near the post office. Then, to the days when my own sons were small and discovered the world.

On other occasions, a woman waiting at a check-out desk would remind me of my mother because of the way she moved or spoke. So it is outside my own life that my past existence lies: in passengers commuting on the subway or the RER; in shoppers glimpsed on escalators at Auchan or in the Galeries Lafayette; in complete strangers who cannot know that they possess part of my story; in faces and bodies which I shall never see again. In the same way, I myself, anonymous among the bustling crowds on streets and in department stores, must secretly play a role in the lives of others.

ABOUT SEVEN STORIES PRESS

SEVEN STORIES PRESS is an independent book publisher based in New York City. We publish works of the imagination by such writers as Nelson Algren, Russell Banks, Octavia E. Butler, Alex DiFrancesco, Ani DiFranco, Assia Djebar, Ariel Dorfman, Annie Ernaux, Coco Fusco, Barry Gifford, Ernesto Che Guevara, Martha Long, Luis Negrón, Peter Plate, Hwang Sok-yong, Lee Stringer, and Kurt Vonnegut, to name a few, together with political titles by voices of conscience, including Subhankar Banerjee, the Boston Women's Health Collective, Noam Chomsky, Angela Y. Davis, Human Rights Watch, Derrick Jensen, Ralph Nader, Loretta Napoleoni, Gary Null, Greg Palast, Project Censored, Barbara Seaman, Alice Walker, Gary Webb, and Howard Zinn, among many others. Seven Stories Press believes publishers have a special responsibility to defend free speech and human rights, and to celebrate the gifts of the human imagination, wherever we can. In 2012 we launched Triangle Square books for young readers with strong social justice and narrative components, telling personal stories of courage and commitment. For additional information, visit www.sevenstories.com.